CABIN CREEK
MYSTERIES

THE CLUE
AT THE BOTTOM
OF THE LAKE

THE CLUE
AT THE BOTTOM
OF THE LAKE

by Kristiana Gregory
illustrated by Patrick Faricy

SCHOLASTIC INC.
New York Toronto London Auckland Sydney
Mexico City New Delhi Hong Kong Buenos Aires

The Clue at the Bottom of the Lake *is*
dedicated to Greg, Cody, and Hailey.

No part of this publication may be reproduced, stored
in a retrieval system, or transmitted in any form or by any means,
electronic, mechanical, photocopying, recording, or otherwise, without
written permission of the publisher. For information regarding permission,
write to Scholastic Inc., Attention: Permissions Department, 557 Broadway,
New York, NY 10012.

ISBN-13: 978-0-439-92951-6
ISBN-10: 0-439-92951-2

12 11 10 9 8 7 6 5 4 3 2 1   8 9 10 11 12 13/0

Printed in the U.S.A.   40

First printing, March 2008

CHAPTERS

1

A Mysterious Splash

The Scottish terrier growled low in his throat. His front paws were on the windowsill as he looked out at the darkness. It was the middle of the night.

Twelve-year-old Jeff Bridger bolted awake, immediately concerned.

"What is it, Rascal?" he whispered.

Through the open bedroom window came the sputtering of a motorboat on the lake. Jeff squinted at the digital clock. What was anyone doing out there at two-thirty in the morning?

He grabbed his binoculars from his bedpost. Then he jumped up to wake his ten-year-old brother, David, who was wrapped in his quilt on the floor. Tessie, their old yellow Lab, was stretched out on David's bed as usual, her head on the pillow. Not bothered by minor disturbances, Tessie slept on.

"David, look! Hurry! A boat's at the island. Something's not right."

David popped up. Still in his T-shirt and shorts from yesterday, he was ready for action. "Okay. I'm awake." He found his binoculars among the clutter of socks and shoes beside him.

In the starlight, the brothers could see Lost Island. Their secret fort was hidden in the island's forest, but they weren't concerned with the fort now. Circling near the rocky point was an aluminum fishing boat that had a shiny stripe along its side. Someone was in the bow, holding up a lantern — the boys couldn't tell if it was a man or a woman. The engine had slowed to a *putter ... putter ... putter*.

Suddenly, a large object was rolled over the side. It splashed into the black water and sank from view. Though half a mile across the lake, the noise was as loud as if from their kitchen downstairs. Jeff and David looked at each other, then raised their binoculars again. Now the boat had been pulled ashore, and someone was walking on the island.

Jeff lowered his voice so he wouldn't wake their mother. "Did that look like someone threw a body overboard?" he asked his younger brother.

"Definitely."

They listened until once again the night was still. Stars wiggled on the surface of the dark lake. Though it seemed peaceful, the boys were uneasy. Jeff reached over a Monopoly game scattered on the carpet for his walkie-talkie.

"We have to let Claire know." He clicked a dial, then held down a button. "Claire?" he whispered into the speaker. "Wake up. Over." He paused a moment, then repeated his message.

Claire was their nine-year-old cousin and best friend. She, too, lived on the lake. Her log home was close enough to Jeff and David's that they could signal each other from their bedroom windows. A footbridge over the creek connected the two properties. When they wanted to talk late at night, the cousins used two-way radios turned down low, so they wouldn't bother their parents. They wished they had cell phones, but there was no reception in these mountains.

Soon, a girl's voice came through the static. "Claire Posey reporting for duty. What's up, guys? Over."

"Suspicious activity," said Jeff. "Will debrief tomorrow. Come to breakfast at seven o'clock sharp.

"Jeff, we were already planning to make pancakes together, remember? Over."

"Oh, right. I forgot. See you tomorrow, then. Over." To David he said, "Now do the secret code."

David aimed his flashlight at Claire's

window. He waved it around, then turned it off and on several times. In response, Claire tugged the strings on her venetian blinds: Open. Shut. Open. Twice. Then, for a grand finale, David smooshed his face against the glass, shining his light up through his nose. At that, Claire closed her blinds.

"What code did you give her?" Jeff asked, getting back into bed.

"Oh, the usual."

"You mean, you made something up?"

"Yep." David returned to his nest on the floor and rolled into his quilt. "Hey, Jeff, what if that really was a body?"

Jeff checked under his pillow to make sure his flashlight was still there. "Well, if it is a body," he replied, "then someone was murdered."

2

First Investigation

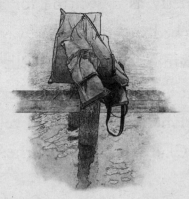

Summer was Jeff and David's favorite time of year. It meant no school for three months.

The next morning, they met Claire by the docks where their families' small boats were tied up. They decided that cooking pancakes for breakfast would take forever. Instead, they stuffed their backpacks with cookies and apples to eat later, such was their hurry to get to the island.

Rascal and Tessie were already in the canoe, sitting quietly as if waiting for a sightseeing tour. Perched in the bow was Yum-Yum, Claire's white poodle. A bell hung from her collar, which jingled every time she turned her head. Her sparkly yellow harness matched Claire's shorts and the laces in her sneakers.

"Ready?" Jeff asked, snapping on a life vest over his clean T-shirt. He adjusted the walkie-talkie on his belt, then sloshed his canteen to make sure it was full. His brown hair was brushed out of his eyes.

"Ready!" said David. He was blond, uncombed, and still wearing the clothes he had slept in.

Because Claire was a redhead and sunburned easily, she wore a baseball cap. Her ponytail hung out the back. "I've got snacks," she said, waving her tiny notebook with her list of things to bring. As usual, her backpack bulged with supplies. Sometimes her planning made the boys impatient, but she had proven to be a worthy ally. They were grateful for her company.

This was the first summer the cousins had permission to explore Lost Island by themselves. Their parents said that as long as they stayed together with the dogs, they didn't have to be home until sunset. Jeff and David's mother was a veterinarian. She worked long hours at the Cabin Creek Animal Hospital. The boys' father, a forest ranger, had died last winter in an accident on Blue Mountain.

Everything the children knew about the wilderness, they had learned from him.

Sunlight reflected off the glassy water as they took turns paddling. Because there was no wind today, their passage took just thirty minutes. After beaching the canoe, they looked back across the lake. Their cabins seemed small and distant. Forest was in every direction, with no roads or neighbors, and the town was several miles away.

"I love being way out here," Claire said.

"Me, too," said David.

Jeff whistled for the dogs, then hefted his backpack. He enjoyed being the leader. "Okay, guys, let's go."

They followed a narrow trail through

scratchy pine and shrubs. Soon they came to the center of the island and the ancient log cabin that was now their fort. They liked the pine tree that happened to be growing inside, up through the roof. Its branches were perfect for hanging up clothes and gear. They stored tiny objects such as Band-Aids and packs of gum in knotholes in the trunk.

One of the old walls had rotted, so the cousins had filled in the gap with a picket fence they'd brought over by boat. A little gate was now their front door.

Seeing that Fort Grizzly Paw hadn't been disturbed by the island's late-night visitor, they took the path to the lookout tower. This was one of the tallest trees on the island, with branches like stair steps. Jeff and David had built a platform up at the top. And with

Claire's help, they had made a pulley system between the fort and tower. This was for delivering supplies and snacks.

"I'll wait here with the dogs," Claire said, clicking on her two-way radio. "Keep me posted. Grandpa gave me a horseshoe from the ranch, so I'm going to find a good place to hang it. They're supposed to bring good luck."

Jeff studied his compass while David took a pencil and some paper from his pack. He sketched a map showing the tip of the island, where they  could see down into the turquoise water. Something white and oblong appeared to be lying on the sandy bottom. It hadn't been there yesterday when they had surveyed the lake from the lookout tower.

"South southeast," Jeff said. "See it there?"

"Yep. Looks easy to swim to. Hey, Jeff . . . in the mud down there, see those footprints? Big man shoes, looks like."

"Uh . . . yeah," Jeff said slowly, focusing his lenses. "There's only one set. Can't be ours, because none of us are ever out there alone."

"Well, *someone's* been here," said David.

Jeff now turned his binoculars toward the far end of the vast lake. Miles away was the Blue Mountain Lodge and Marina. Tourist and fishing boats were launched from there. As Jeff's gaze followed the bike path into town, he said, "Uh-oh."

David took a look, then said, "Claire will want to know about this!"

Jeff was already tuning his walkie-talkie. "Claire, do you read? Come in. Over."

"Here I am. What d'you see? Over." She was at the base of the tree, so the boys could hear her voice from below and also through the radio's speaker.

"Change of plans. We're leaving the island ASAP. Over."

"Why as soon as possible? Over."

"Cop cars with flashing lights are in the park. Yellow police tape. Over."

David was in too much of a hurry to use his radio. He shouted down to Claire, "Something's up. I bet it has to do with that boat we saw last night. Probably a murder."

3

A Puzzling Clue

The town of Cabin Creek was in the mountains on a beautiful lake. It was usually peaceful, but today there seemed to be trouble. The cousins canoed back to their dock, then jumped on their bikes. The shortcut through the woods soon brought them to Main Street. They had left Rascal at home with old Tessie, but Yum-Yum rode in the basket on Claire's handlebars, her dainty bell ringing over every bump.

As they neared the park, they could see a crowd of people, mostly little kids. Yellow streamers surrounded the picnic area. Balloons floated above the jungle gym and swings. A clown was twirling a hula hoop while juggling green tennis balls. His orange wig hung down to his shoulders.

Claire coasted her bike to a stop. "You guys, it's just day camp," she said, disappointed. "I went here last summer. This is the party for their first day."

"But I saw police cars with flashing lights," Jeff said.

"And I heard a siren," said David, also disappointed.

A man grilling hamburgers on a barbecue waved to the cousins. He wore a white jacket and tall white hat. It was their good friend

Mr. Henry, the prized chef from the Blue Mountain Lodge. He was famous for his pastries, especially pecan pie. They had known him from the years he worked at the café in town, which was owned by Claire's parents. Mr.  Henry loved children, so every summer he volunteered to help at day camp, and the Lodge donated all the food.

"Hello, my friends!" he called. "Come, Yum-Yum." The poodle pranced over to him, sat on her haunches, then lifted her front paw. It was her polite way of asking for the treat he always had in his pocket. Mr. Henry patted her curly white head.

"Here you go," he said. "So what brings you kids to the park? Hey, knock it off!" he said to the clown who had sneaked up behind him. He was squirting the chef with a giant water pistol. "I told you twice already to cut it out."

Turning back to the cousins, Mr. Henry said, "Now, where were we?"

Jeff explained about the police and the siren. Meanwhile, David unzipped his pack and took out his sketch pad to draw the picnic. He didn't have a camera, so this was his way of keeping a journal.

"Indeed, police were here," answered Mr. Henry. "Some teenagers in a sports car were zipping through town. But the cops stopped 'em right in front of the park and gave the driver a speeding ticket. Now they're gone."

"Well, that answers *that*," said Claire.

"Will you stay for lunch?" the chef asked. "We have plenty."

"Thank you, anyway, Mr. Henry. We're on our way to the café."

The chef nodded. "Be sure to say hi to your folks for me."

After David finished his drawing, the cousins rode along the bike path to the Western Café. Claire's parents were friendly to everyone. Aunt Lilly was plump and pretty, with red hair like her daughter. Uncle Wyatt wore a cowboy hat and cowboy boots and was always ready with a smile. He led the children to a booth with a view of the lake. Other than their fort on the island, this was their favorite place for serious meetings.

"The usual?" Uncle Wyatt asked. He would be happy to cook anything they wanted, but they always ordered the same thing: cheeseburgers and chocolate shakes.

"Yes, please!" they answered.

The cousins scooted close to one another to whisper. After a waitress brought their food, they got down to business.

Claire looked up from under the brim of her baseball cap. "You guys guessed wrong about the flashing lights in the park. And the police tape just turned out to be yellow streamers. So, are you *sure* you *really* saw a body get dumped overboard last night? Tell me again. *Every single detail.*"

"It was a body," said Jeff, trying to sound sure of himself.

"Definitely," David agreed. He was peeling apart his burger to stuff it with potato chips. "Why else would someone go all the way out to Lost Island in the middle of the night?"

"Then shouldn't we tell the police?"

The brothers looked at each other.

"Well, maybe it *wasn't* a body," David answered, feeling embarrassed. What if he and his brother had guessed wrong, after all?

"Come to think of it," Jeff said, "it probably wasn't. Let's watch the news tonight. If there's been no robbery or murder, we —"

Their voices were drowned out by teenagers at the next table. They recognized Rex McCoy as one of the busboys from the Lodge dining room. He also worked at the army surplus store. He and his younger brother, Ronald, were mean and often bullied their classmates — including the cousins.

"I sneaked out of the house last night," Rex boasted. "My dad still doesn't know I took his boat. Yee-haw, what a blast! Except for one little problem . . ."

At the mention of the boat, the cousins kicked one another under the table.

Suddenly, Rex looked over at them. "You there," he said. "Me and Ronald are keeping an eye on you little shrimps. So don't get any ideas. Ha-ha."

The cousins left the café for home. They rode through the woods as fast as they could.

"The McCoys are still at it!" David cried. "If they find our fort, they'll smash it up."

Claire was pedaling hard over the dirt path, which was bumpy with pinecones and twigs. "Guys," she said, trying to keep up with them, "what if Rex is the one from last night who dumped something in the lake? He and Ronald could be up to something terrible."

Ronald McCoy was Claire's age and in her class. "Before school was out, Ronald stole my purple pen," she told her cousins. "When I snatched it off his desk, he punched me in the arm. I don't trust those McCoys."

"Me, neither," said Jeff. "But first things first. We've gotta find out what's at the bottom of the lake. ASAP."

4

Just Like a Body

It was one o'clock in the hot afternoon by the time the cousins came through the woods to their cabins. They changed into their swim-suits and canoed to the island with the dogs.

On the far shore, they inspected the stranger's footprints up close. They could also see scrapes in the mud where a small boat had been beached.

"Whoever was here didn't go very far," Jeff said, pointing to the ground. "And there's definitely only one pair of shoe prints, not two. Maybe it was Rex. At least he didn't go looking for our fort."

"Good!" David yelled. "Let's take a swim!" He peeled off his shirt and twirled it in the air, letting it flutter to the sand.

Jeff, however, folded his T-shirt on top of his sneakers before running after his brother. "Right behind you!" he called. "But don't forget what Dad told us."

This was an alpine lake, filled by snow melting high in the mountains. Even during the hottest months of summer, it didn't warm up. Dad had taught them *never* to dive headfirst into a river or pond — you might hit submerged logs or boulders. Another danger was the sudden cold. It could make your heart stop and you could drown.

It was safest to wade in slowly, as Jeff began doing. But the sun was hot, and David had seen the area from the lookout tower. He thought it was safe and was in too much of a hurry to cool off. Calling Rascal, he raced from the sand and splashed in with a cannonball. The black Scottie trotted in after him.

David screamed when he came up for air. "It's freezing!"

By now, Claire had unlaced her sneakers and was tiptoeing into the lake. Yum-Yum followed her. But the poodle immediately backed up when her dainty paws felt the cold water.

"It's ice!" Claire yelled. She swam, head held high, until directly over the mysterious object. She looked down, allowing just the tip of her nose to be in the water. At this curious angle — just inches above the surface — she could see as clearly as if wearing a face mask. This was something else the boys' dad had taught them.

"There it is!" she cried. "It looks like a white duffel bag. And it's not too deep. I'm getting out. It's *toooo* cold."

"Okay, here I go," said Jeff. Now up to his waist, he took several quick breaths, then a deep one, before swimming down toward the sandy bottom. Whining with worry, Tessie kept her eye on Jeff.

Claire and David also were concerned. They watched him go deeper and deeper. For one terrible moment it seemed as if Jeff had stopped moving. David threw his towel to the ground, ready to dive in after his brother.

Then, suddenly, Jeff was there, pawing for the surface. He gasped for air. David reached out his hand and helped him to the beach. Claire brought him a towel.

"It's really, really cold down there," Jeff said, still trying to catch his breath. He shook his wet hair out of his eyes. "Could hardly move my arms, they were getting numb so fast. I grabbed the bag, but it's heavy. Didn't budge an inch. We need to go home and get our wet suits so we don't freeze to death. Whatever that thing is, it's heavy and lumpy."

David's eyes were wide. "Lumpy like a body," he whispered.

It was late afternoon by the time the cousins canoed home. They settled in the sunroom of the Bridger cabin, which faced the lake. A small TV was in the corner. They crowded onto a couch with their dogs to watch the five o'clock news. So far, no robberies or missing people had been reported.

Jeff switched the remote to another channel. A basketball game. *Click.* Cooking show. *Click.* Politics. *Click.* Cartoons. "Huh," he said, clicking it off. "Maybe the police are keeping quiet."

"They do that?" asked David.

"I saw it on a detective show once," Claire explained. "Sometimes they don't announce crimes. That way a bad guy might blab about stuff only he and the cops know. Then they can put him in jail."

The cousins stayed on the couch with their dogs sprawled over their laps. They watched the lake turn orange from the setting sun. Lost Island soon became a shadow.

"Tomorrow," said Jeff.

"Seven o'clock sharp," said David.

"Mission Recovery," said Claire.

5

Mission Recovery

On the island the next morning, the cousins climbed their lookout tower. They could see that the object at the bottom of the lake had not been moved since yesterday.

"It's smaller than I thought," Jeff said, looking through his binoculars.

Claire looked through hers and agreed. "Maybe it's a big pillow or something?"

Jeff shook his head. "It looked too heavy when it hit the water to be a pillow."

"So how're we gonna fish it out?" David asked.

"Guys, I've got an idea." Claire was already climbing down from the high platform. The boys followed her to Fort Grizzly Paw. It was stocked with supplies they had ferried across the lake: lumber scraps, a toolbox, ropes, pulleys, a camouflage tarp, camping gear, and assorted junk they might need.

After explaining her plan, Claire and the boys stuffed their daypacks with odds and ends, then hiked to the shore, five minutes away. There they set to work. Using a pair of pliers, Claire turned a wire coat hanger into a giant hook. Jeff secured it to a long stretch of fishing line. Then David filled one of his socks with sand to use for a sinker, tying it below the hook.

Now they tied the other end to a tree. This way, it wouldn't slip away from them. They looked out at the lake to make sure no one was watching.

Jeff volunteered to start their operation. First, he squeezed into the tight shirt of his wet suit. It had long sleeves and zipped up to his neck in back. Then he swam down and hooked the bag. He surfaced, his legs goose-bumply from the freezing water.

"Got it!" Jeff cried. "Pull slowly."

But in the excitement, David gave a yank. The wire came undone and sank to the bottom.

"Why'd you do that?" Jeff cried. "Now we have to start all over." He got out and flopped down in the warm sand, shivering. "That lake is *so* cold. Even in this rubber shirt."

"I'm sorry, Jeff," said David. "Let's try again. I'll go in next."

Claire had brought extra hangers, so she made another hook for David's attempt. Unfortunately, this one also fell off the line and sank from sight. It was her turn next. She wiggled into her wet-suit top, the neon green one she wore when waterskiing with her parents. But when the boys pulled the line, the hanger broke in two.

After three hours, the cousins decided to rest. They sat on logs of driftwood, towels around their shoulders. While warming up in the sunshine, they fortified themselves with animal crackers. They drank from their canteens.

"We can't give up," they encouraged one another.

"Hey," cried Claire, digging through her pack. "I just remembered something!

"Ta-da!" she cried, holding up the iron horseshoe. There were tiny holes so it could be nailed onto a horse's hoof. "I didn't find a place for it in the fort, so I brought it for good luck. Let's try it. A horseshoe's not going to snap in two, that's for sure."

They threaded fishing line through one of the holes, then secured it with their favorite triple knot. They wound the other end of the line through a pulley the size of an Oreo cookie, then tied it to a tree. Next, David put on his wet suit. He swam down into the frigid water. Claire and Jeff watched as he hooked the horseshoe to the bag's rope. A few seconds later, he burst to the surface.

"Ready!" he yelled, splashing his arms for shore.

The smooth wheel of the pulley kept the line from snagging. The horseshoe held firm. At long last, inch by inch, the cousins were able to drag their discovery up through the clear water to the muddy shore. It was heavy, the size of a waterlogged sleeping bag. They stood and stared. Waves lapped against its bulky side.

David pushed it with his foot. There was a clinking noise, like metal.

"Doesn't sound like bones," he said.

They took off their wet suits and looked out at the lake. Though it was late afternoon, there were no boats in sight.

"So, who wants to inspect it first?" Jeff asked. He opened his pocketknife and slit the rope. Water gushed out of the bag as its mouth gaped open.

Claire knelt in the wet sand to peek inside. "No dead body. Just a bunch of towels wrapped up and tied with string." She pulled out one of the bundles, then David used his knife to cut away the ties.

Several metal bowls rolled out.

"Huh," Claire said. "These are like what Mom and Dad use at the café for mixing potato salad and coleslaw."

"That can't be it," David insisted. "There has to be something besides old bowls."

The cousins were quiet, wondering what to do next.

"Maybe we should get the bag home," David finally suggested. "Then we can take our time inspecting it. To see if there's any treasure."

Claire rubbed her arms. She was starting to shiver from her swim in the cold lake and said, "But it won't fit in the canoe with all of us."

"And it's almost sunset," Jeff observed. "There's not enough time to make two trips." Shadows from the trees were darkening the island. The mountain air was quickly cooling off. They put on their sweatshirts and pondered their predicament.

"I know!" said David. "Let's take it to the fort, where it'll be safe. Then first thing in the morning, we'll come here with the caboose."

The caboose was the old rowboat they often towed behind their canoe to haul equipment. Three kids, three dogs, and all their gear could safely make the trip together in the two craft.

"But what if someone comes back for it tonight?" Claire worried. "If Rex McCoy dropped this thing overboard, he's not going to be happy that it's gone. He might search around. If they find it in the fort, they might trace it to us."

"That's for sure," said David.

Jeff again looked at the sky. "We'll hide it behind the cabin, under Dad's old tarp. You know, the green-and-brown one we brought from home? No one will look there. But we better hurry. The sun's goin' down fast."

6

A Curious Discovery

The cousins spent an anxious night camped in the Bridger sunroom. All the windows were open so they could hear any motorboats on the lake. But the night was quiet.

At dawn they woke to the back door closing as Mom left for work. Since they had slept in their clothes, they crawled out of their bags and tiptoed from the cabin down to the dock. While the dogs drank from the lake, the kids gathered their gear.

No one said a word. An important mission such as this didn't require chitchat.

So, in hooded sweatshirts to protect against the early morning chill, the cousins took up their paddles.

It was almost noon by the time they were able to haul the bag home. Even though it had been out of the lake overnight, it still oozed with water. It dripped from their fort to the rowboat, then along the dock, to their cabin, through the kitchen, and up the bumpy stairs.

The boys' bedroom was littered with clothing, shoes, games, and model airplane parts, mostly David's mess. Jeff had one shelf where his fossil collection and dead bugs were neatly arranged.

The cousins had agreed to conduct their investigation here rather than at Claire's cabin. Aunt Lilly kept a tidy house and would know if something peculiar had arrived. The boys' mother, however, was less fussy about the odd things her sons brought home.

Water seeped onto the hardwood floor. It smelled fishy from the lake. The boys dried the floor with wads of socks and T-shirts. They didn't want their mother to be startled by a wet trail in the hallway.

Jeff loosened the rope around the bag. Now David and Claire pulled from the other end, as if emptying a pillowcase. With a loud thump, out rolled several items wrapped in soggy towels.

"All right!" said David. "Let's open 'em up."

*   *   *

The cousins stared at an assortment of bowls and platters. Their disappointment was huge.

"Bunch of junk," David said.

"That's for sure," said Jeff.

Claire examined one of the platters. "Mom uses one like this at Thanksgiving, for serving the big ol' turkey."

"Is it valuable?" Jeff asked. "I mean, if these are stolen, could the robber sell them for a lot of money?"

"No way. They're big pie tins, that's all."

While Claire and Jeff continued their inspection, David uncovered a flat jewelry box wrapped in plastic. Carefully, he opened the lid. It was dry inside. He expected to see a necklace, but instead there was a knife encased in velvet. Its blade was eight inches long, and the handle was covered with beautiful carvings of animals: a moose and grizzly bear on one side, a buffalo on the other.

"Huh," David said to himself. Something bothered him about these carvings. They were very familiar. He pulled out his sketch pad from under his mattress and began drawing, trying to remember where he'd seen them.

Meanwhile, his brother and cousin were by the window. They were holding a platter to the light, trying to read some words engraved in the metal. They didn't notice David with the knife.

"Hello!" came a voice from downstairs. "Boys? Claire?"

The brothers jumped up. *Mom's home early!* They could hear her footsteps coming up to their room. With a quick sweep of their arms, Jeff and Claire buried things under a pile of clothes, then pushed them into the closet. David shoved the knife under his mattress with his drawings.

Just then, Dr. Daisy Bridger stood in the doorway, smiling. She had David's blue eyes and blond hair, which she wore in a long braid over her shoulder. "I brought sandwiches from the café," she said. "Let's eat in the sunroom, where there's a breeze."

"Thanks, Mom. We'll be right down."

"Thanks, Aunt Daisy."

The brothers sighed with relief. If Mom had seen their discovery, she would wonder how they found it. It would mean explaining the mysterious boat at night. Mom would then tell her sister, Aunt Lilly, who would tell Uncle Wyatt. Then they would sit down over cups of coffee and probably change their minds about the kids going to Lost Island.

The cousins didn't want their parents to think it was dangerous out there.

A basket of potato chips was on the low coffee table. Mom unwrapped roast beef sandwiches and put them on plates, handing every child a napkin and an apple. They sat on the floor.

"So how's your day going?" Mom asked. Her face and arms were tanned from working outside with horses. She often drove to the nearby ranches to doctor the larger animals.

"Good," her sons answered. They shrugged as if it were just a regular day.

"We took the canoe out this morning," Claire said.

"That sounds like fun, kids. What else do you have planned for —"

"Oh, nothing special," Jeff replied. He hadn't meant to interrupt his mother but he had noticed something on the lake. So had David and Claire.

An aluminum fishing boat was approaching Lost Island.

Sid the Rooster

The cousins tried not to show their alarm. They hurriedly ate their lunch while glancing out the window. The boat seemed identical to the other night's. It even had something shiny painted on its side, but without their binoculars they couldn't tell if it was the same stripe.

The boys' mom noticed them staring out at the water. "That's odd," she said. "Tourists rarely come this far, especially this early in the summer."

"Uh . . . wonder who it could be?" Jeff asked. He felt uneasy and hoped they wouldn't have to tell Mom the whole story. Not yet, anyway. While she was looking out at the boat, he sneaked some roast beef under the table to Tessie.

David, too, was nervous. He gave Rascal a slice of tomato.

"Maybe, uh, a fisherman?" Claire said, slipping Yum-Yum the rest of her sandwich.

"Hm. Doubtful," Mom replied. "Not many know how to navigate through all the little islands and coves. That's why people get lost so easily. Your dad used to get called for search and rescues all the time, boys. Anyway, that's why our two families built our cabins here. It's peaceful. Well, I need to get over to the Double R Ranch. You kids mind cleaning this —?"

"We're on it, Mom!" Jeff jumped up, gathering the paper plates and napkins. Claire crunched the soda cans into the kitchen's recycling box, and David brushed crumbs off the table to the waiting dogs.

"Okay, then," Mom said. "See you for dinner." The car keys jingled in her hand as she waved good-bye. Then she cast a parting smile at the three dogs cleaning up the floor.

The cousins watched the lake as they rode their bikes through the woods, along the shoreline trail. To their relief, the fishing boat had turned around before it reached Lost Island. It was now weaving its way among the small isles, back toward town.

"Hurry," said Jeff. "Maybe we can get to the docks in time to see who it is."

"Race you!" David cried, pedaling fast, Claire close behind.

But when they arrived at the Marina, there were several aluminum boats already tied up. One had a shiny blue stripe along its hull. There was no way to tell how long the boat had been there. A fisherman was on the wharf looking through his tackle box with a little boy. Two women were getting into a canoe, and a man was docking his small sailboat. No one seemed to have just come in off the lake.

"Let's hang around for a while," Jeff said. "We might find a clue."

They took off their shoes and sat on the sandy beach. The cousins liked watching the families who vacationed in their mountains. People rented paddleboats, bicycles, and fishing gear. Grandparents pushed baby strollers, and there were kids on Rollerblades. The swimming beach was crowded despite the cold lake. Everyone seemed cheerful.

"No one looks suspicious," David observed.

"Well, I have a theory," said Jeff. Since turning twelve, he liked having theories. "Maybe someone was cleaning out a shed. Then, for some weird reason, he drove one of these boats all the way to Lost Island to dump everything."

"So who was that we saw out there today?" Claire asked. "The same person?"

"Maybe a sightseer," said David. "Hey, guys, since there was nothing valuable in the sack, do we need to tell the police?" For the moment, he had forgotten about the beautiful knife he had hidden.

The cousins gave one another a questioning look. "I'm not sure," Jeff replied. "Maybe after we figure out some of these clues."

Claire reached into her pocket. "Like the one we just found. Here, I wrote it down." She handed a piece of paper to David. On it were three words: *Sid the Rooster.*

"Who's Sid the Rooster?" David asked.

"That's what we were wondering," said Jeff. "His name is engraved on that platter."

"I bet it's someone famous." Claire swished her red ponytail over her shoulder like a movie star.

Now David remembered the knife. He wanted to tell Jeff and Claire, but suddenly, he liked having his very own secret. Earlier in the summer he and his brother had found a skeleton foot on the island. He had wanted to display it in their bedroom, but Jeff insisted they bury it. David wanted this knife to be his secret for a little while longer.

"David!" Claire said. She and Jeff had put on their shoes and were hurrying toward the Lodge.

"Huh?"

"Come on," she called. "Someone's arguing in the Lodge."

The hotel manager, Miss Allen, wagged her finger at Mr. Henry, the chef. She was wearing a white blouse, a black skirt, and pointy black shoes. Her hair was up in a bun.

"This is the third time you've brought it up today," she cried, "and the answer is still no!"

Miss Allen stormed out of the kitchen, muttering to herself. The cousins heard her whisper, *"...going to Italy soon as I've got the money."* They were shocked to see her so angry at Mr. Henry. It was well known she adored him for his delicious desserts, which had made the Lodge famous in the two years he had worked there. "Oh, pardon me!" she said, startled to see the cousins by the cash register. "May I show you to a table?"

"Yes, please," was Claire's quick response. "Over there, with that gentleman."

"You mean Grumpy Gus?" the woman asked.

All eyes turned to a table by the window where an elderly man was doing a crossword puzzle. He had white hair and a white beard. The remains of his lunch were being cleared by a waitress.

Jeff and David wondered what their cousin was up to. Grumpy Gus had been their father's hiking buddy and close friend. He was their friend, too. They called him Mr. Wellback because of the way he started the stories he told them about when he was a kid.

"I'm warning you," said Miss Allen, "he doesn't tolerate any nonsense. And neither do I." She lifted her chin, looking down at David's messy hair and mismatched socks. He was still wearing yesterday's clothes. Jeff, however, had changed his shirt after their lunch with Mom. Claire's purple baseball cap matched her sneakers, which made her look organized.

"Well," said Miss Allen, "at least *two* of you are presentable. Follow me." She grabbed three children's menus — the paper kind to draw on — and a jar of crayons.

Mr. Wellback looked up from his puzzle and removed his spectacles. He didn't smile.

"Do your parents know where you are?" he asked them.

"Yes, sir. We always leave a note."

He motioned for them to take a seat.

"What sort of trouble are you scallywags stirring up this time?" he asked.

Claire took a deep breath. Her green eyes narrowed. "Suspicious activity, sir," she said. "Since you've been in Cabin Creek a long time, we have a question for you."

"I haven't got all day, child."

"Do you know anyone named Sid the Rooster?"

Now Mr. Wellback narrowed *his* eyes. "Do I look like a farmer to you?"

"No, sir."

"Never heard of the fella. What's this all about?"

The cousins were quiet. They glanced at one another, wondering if they should tell Mr. Wellback about their discovery. After some fidgeting, Claire said, "We found something with writing on it. I copied down the words." Then she showed him the piece of paper.

The old man put on his glasses. "You want to tell me what's really going on?"

Again the children looked uneasy. They didn't answer.

"Well, back when I was a boy," he said, after a long silence, "everyone had a front porch. In those days, a person could always share a secret on a friend's porch." He paused before looking at each kid. "By the way, I'm up at dawn every single morning." He pointed to their menus.

"Now, if you rabble-rousers are hungry, order something," he said. "I'll tell Miss Allen to put it on my tab."

With that, Mr. Wellback stood up and left, taking the crayons with him. He did not approve of how Miss Allen had treated the cousins like little children.

8

On Mr. Wellback's Porch

At sunrise the next morning, the cousins hiked to Mr. Wellback's cabin, twenty minutes away and up a twisty road. Several hound dogs were napping on his porch. Through the trees was a view of the lake and Lost Island. The old man studied the platter they had brought him, turning it over and over, rubbing spots with his thumb.

"First off," he said, "this isn't a tin pan. It's a serving tray. And the reason it's black is because it's tarnished. This is sterling silver. Do you whippersnappers know what that means?"

Jeff nodded his head yes as David shook his head no. Claire shrugged, trying to guess.

"It's worth money, that's what. Now, where'd you see that name, young lady?"

Claire showed him. Mr. Wellback ran his fingers over the engraving. Then he tilted it to catch the sunlight slanting in by his chair.

"Hmm. Bunch of letters have worn away. Can hardly see 'em, but I'll tell you this much. There's a whole phrase here, and this part does not spell *Sid the Rooster.*"

"It doesn't?"

Pointing to David's sketch pad, he said, "Sonny, can you spare a scrap of paper and your pencil?"

"Yes, sir!" said David, eager to help.

The old man drew a dotted line across the page. "You kids ever play hangman, the word game? Lots of blanks, and you try to figure out a word?"

"Yeah. I like it better than Monopoly," Claire offered. "It's quicker."

"That it is, missy. Now watch." He filled in some of the blanks with letters, then showed it to them:

T H E _ _ _ _ _   R O O S _ _ _ _ _

Mr. Wellback tapped the pencil against his head in concentration. "It's a puzzle, all right."

Suddenly, he gave a deep laugh. "Well, I'll be."

"What? What?"

"Okay, I'll help you with the name, but the rest you'll have to figure out yourself. Ask me for a letter."

"You mean like in hangman?"

"That's exactly what I mean."

The cousins started calling out letters. One by one, Mr. Wellback filled in a *D*, three *E*s, a *T*, and so on. Now he showed them the paper.

Claire read, *"Theodore Roosevelt?"*

"Yes."

The cousins were quiet for a moment. Then David said, "Who's Theodore Roosevelt?"

Mr. Wellback dropped his head to his chest, groaning. "Honest to Pete, it makes my toes curl to think you kids aren't paying attention in school."

"Sounds familiar," said Jeff. David and Claire squinted as they, too, tried to place the name.

The old man took a deep breath. "I don't know where you found this silver tray or what you plan to do with it, but here's what *we're* going to do. *You* rascals are going to the library — it opens in ten minutes. *I* am going to enjoy my second cup of coffee. After you've learned about Theodore Roosevelt, let's meet on the trail to my cabin, say, eleven o'clock. Be sure to bring your canteens."

"Canteens?"

"That's right. We're going on a hike."

9

Up the Twisty Road

The library was next to the park and baseball field. Though it was a hot day, the cousins ignored the ice cream kiosk in front and hurried into the building. They were eager to see where the clue *Theodore Roosevelt* might lead them.

On the computer, they typed in the name, jotted down the reference number, then went to the nonfiction shelves. When they found the title they were looking for, they took it to a table, searched the index, and started reading. The library was quiet except for two teenage girls next to  them, giggling over a magazine.

Twenty minutes later, the cousins returned the book. As they rode their bikes home, they discussed the notes David had written for them on his sketch pad.

"Okay," Jeff began, "when President

McKinley was assassinated, his vice president took over."

"That was Theodore Roosevelt," said Claire. "People called him Teddy. In fact, the teddy bear was named after him."

David's notes were in his backpack, but he remembered the details. "At age forty-two," he recited, "Theodore Roosevelt became the twenty-sixth president of the United States, the youngest ever."

"In the year nineteen hundred and one," Claire added. "Good, we're home! Here's the creek."

Their tires thumped and bumped as they rode over the wooden footbridge, then they dropped their bikes on the lawn.

"Let's go look at those plates again," said Jeff. "Maybe there's another clue."

　　　　　*　　　*　　　*

The brothers cleared a space in the center of their room and dragged the bag from their closet. With Claire's help, they tried to polish the engravings, to make them easier to read. Soon they realized that the twelve silver bowls in various sizes and the eight silver platters were all engraved. The words had faded in different spots, but they all appeared to say the same thing. They wrote down what words they could decipher.

After some minutes, Claire whooped. "Now I get it! Look, guys." She showed the brothers her puzzle.

A GIFT FROM ___SID___
THE_____ ROOS_____

"Still looks like *Sid the Rooster*," Jeff said.

Claire pointed her pencil to the letters. *"A Gift from President Theodore Roosevelt,"* she read. "See?"

David tilted his head to read the side of a bowl. "Oh, yeah. Here's the word *Gift*," he said.

The cousins pondered this new development.

"New theory," Jeff said. "These might be valuable. Maybe whoever dumped them in the lake planned to fish them out later and sell them."

"But what are gifts from President Roosevelt doing in Cabin Creek?" Claire asked.

"Maybe Mr. Wellback knows," David answered.

"I'll fill up the canteens," said Jeff.

Claire headed downstairs to the kitchen. "And I'll get some snacks."

*   *   *

Mr. Wellback leaned on his hiking stick and pointed up the hill. His water bottle was strapped across his shoulder. "Enjoy listening to the birds," he told the cousins, "and don't bother me with questions until we get to the top."

"The *top*?"

"Yes, sir. Your dad and I would do this on his lunch hour. Come along."

Hiking up a mountain on a hot morning wasn't the brothers' idea of fun. But they tried to be cheerful, knowing their father had taken this path. Besides, Claire was way ahead of them, walking with the old man as if the pair did this every day. She was even swinging her arms with gusto.

After several stops to drink water and share granola bars, the group reached a plateau. The trail opened up to a large flat boulder, where Mr. Wellback took a seat. Before them was a sweeping view of the lake and distant mountain range. High white clouds adorned the blue sky. The breeze brought an aroma of sagebrush.

Some minutes later, he said, "Theodore Roosevelt loved this view."

"He was *here*?"

"Sat on this very rock."

"How do you know?"

"Remember I told you about my way-back grandpa, the famous gunslinger Sheriff Gus Penny?"

"Yes, sir."

"He had three brothers. Mountain men,

tough as they come. Well, back in 1891, Teddy Roosevelt came west. He liked adventure and hunting, so the Penny brothers guided him into our rugged mountains. When they weren't camping in tents, they stayed at the Blue Mountain Lodge. Fact, the stuffed buffalo head above the fireplace is from those fellows. You've seen it plenty of times. One of those ol' boys kept a journal, that's how I know about this rock."

"Wow," they exclaimed.

"So," Mr. Wellback continued, "I suspect that after Mr. Roosevelt was elected to the White House, he sent that silver platter as a thank-you gift. Polite people do that sort of thing."

Again the cousins were quiet. They glanced at one another, then Jeff said, "There is more than one platter."

Mr. Wellback turned on the rock to look at them. "What d'you mean, more?"

All at once the kids began describing the boat in the middle of the night, swimming for the bag, then how the items all had some kind of inscription.

David, however, still didn't mention the knife. Being reminded of the buffalo head in the Lodge had given him a jolt. He remembered where he'd seen the identical animals on the knife's handle, and it made him feel dreadful. Now there was another reason he wasn't ready to tell the others about the knife.

After hearing their story, Mr. Wellback whistled through his teeth. "Enough serving bowls and platters for a banquet?"

"We thought it was just a bunch of junk," said Claire.

"Well, guess what. It isn't."

"So they're valuable?"

"*Valuable!* Is that lake down there full of water?"

Jeff hesitated. "How much, do you think?"

Mr. Wellback whistled again. "Personal gifts from a president of the United States? From more than a century ago? And sterling silver? I venture to guess thousands of dollars."

"*Thousands?*"

"At least. Maybe more."

"More?"

"That's right. Whoever dumped that bag knew they were hiding priceless antiques, that's for ding-dong sure. Why no one has reported them missing is another mystery. I'd say the police should know about this."

Mr. Wellback gazed out at the mountains. He shook his head. "The thieves'll be spittin' mad that it's not there anymore." His voice trailed off.

"I've been warning you to be careful on Lost Island. It's brought nothing but trouble for years and years."

10

Emergency Meeting

The hike down the mountain took fifteen minutes. After the cousins thanked Mr. Wellback and said good-bye, they ran the rest of the way home. They grabbed bags of trail mix for lunch, then went down to the water with the dogs.

"Emergency meeting," Jeff said, pacing along the shore. "*Now* we should tell the cops."

"But what about the thief?" asked David. "If he sees the bag is missing and looks across the lake at our canoe, he might suspect us. There'll be trouble for sure. Like Mr. Wellback said."

Claire climbed onto the dock and grabbed their life vests from a post. "Let's make a decoy before we go to the police," she said. "If we take that duffel to the island, we can fill it with rocks, then dump it where we found it. That way, if the thief *does* check on the bag, he'll see it's still at the bottom of the lake and think everything is safe. What d'you say?"

"I'll go get it," David called. Already he was running up the beach to their cabin. He was glad to stop thinking about the knife under his mattress.

Jeff started gathering the oars. "I don't know what we'd do without you, Claire."

*   *   *

It was easier to return the heavy bag to the lake than it had been to retrieve it. The cousins sat in their canoe and looked down into the water.

"Almost a perfect landing," David said.

"Now we wait," said Claire.

"And watch for the thief to come back," Jeff said.

Crackling from Claire's walkie-talkie interrupted them. "Daddy?" she answered. "Is everything okay? Over." She knew he was nearby because their radios had only a two-mile radius.

"Everything's fine, honey," came Uncle Wyatt's voice. "We have a surprise for you guys. Time to come home. Over."

Uncle Wyatt was waiting for them on the dock. He bent down to help old Tessie out of the canoe. Rascal and Yum-Yum leaped out on their own.

"What's the surprise, Dad?"

"Grandma and Grandpa finished their new stables. They've invited you to the ranch for a few days."

"Awesome," said Jeff and David.

"I can't wait!" Claire said. "When?"

"The bus leaves at six o'clock sharp," her father answered.

Claire's mouth dropped open. She looked at her watch. "But that's in an hour."

"Yep." He gave her ponytail a playful tug. "Grandma just phoned. You know how she likes arranging things at the last minute. Don't worry, you'll be there in time for supper. Barbecued ribs and corn on the cob."

The cousins hurried to their cabins to pack.

They loved visiting their grandparents but were frustrated they wouldn't be home to guard the island. And there wasn't time to take the serving dishes to the police.

"We'll have to wait until we get back," said Jeff. "At least everything's safe in our closet. And the decoy's in the lake."

Uncle Wyatt drove the cousins to the bus stop, which was in front of the Blue Mountain Lodge. After they had unloaded their sleeping bags and backpacks, he hugged them, waved good-bye with his cowboy hat, then returned to the café.

Jeff, David, and Claire set their gear down and stood with a group of tourists also waiting for the bus. They were startled to see the

McCoy boys walk by, carrying fishing poles and tackle boxes. The McCoys didn't notice the cousins among the crowd.

"I was gonna buy me a truck," Rex was saying to his little brother. "But now I gotta quick use the money to get a new —"

Vrrooom . . . vrrooom came the bus with its loud rumbling engine.

The cousins climbed aboard and gave their tickets to the driver. They rushed to the long seat in back, where they could sit together and look out the rear window.

"Did you hear that?" David said. He took out his sketch pad to draw the McCoy brothers heading to the docks.

"Sure did," said Claire.

"New theory," said Jeff. "Rex McCoy knows about those antiques because he works at the Lodge. And for some reason he needs money."

Now the cousins had another surprise. As the bus pulled away from the Lodge, a woman ran out. She was calling to someone by the lake.

"That's Miss Allen!" the cousins said. The last thing they saw as their bus rounded a corner was Miss Allen shaking hands with Rex and Ronald McCoy.

"Are they partners?" Claire asked. "Remember, we heard her say she's going to Italy as soon as she gets the money."

David was still drawing and didn't answer. He felt a quiet relief about these suspects. He might not need to tell about the knife, after all.

"Wow," said Jeff. "So maybe Miss Allen got Rex to drive the duffel out to Lost Island. He dumped the bag, then walked onshore for some reason — remember the big footprints? He's tall. They could have been his."

Claire gave her cousins a worried look. "What if they go out there while we're gone?"

11

A Dreadful Mistake

The cousins had been going to Lucky Bridger Ranch ever since they were little. It was their favorite place away from Cabin Creek. Their grandparents let them ride horses along the sunny trails and taught them how to rope a calf. The kids helped clean stables and groom the animals.

All weekend they wondered about the crime. And at night, in the bunkhouse, they discussed their theories.

"Now we know why there was nothing in the news about a robbery," Jeff said from his sleeping bag. He was lying on his back with his hands behind his head as he thought about things.

David agreed. "Since Rex and Miss Allen work at the Lodge, they could sneak all that silver out. They're probably the only ones who know it's missing."

"Hey, guys," Claire said. "Remember when we were in the café and Rex bragged about taking his dad's boat?"

"Yeah?"

"Well, he said it was fun, except he'd had a 'little problem.' D'you think he used it that night but ran onto the rocks or something, and that's why he needs money? To fix it?"

David sat up in his bunk. "*Yeah* . . . the

other day by the bus stop, remember we heard him tell his slimy little brother that he can't use the money for a truck anymore?"

"He probably needs to fix that boat before his dad finds out," said Jeff. "Okay. How 'bout this? When we get home, we'll go to Lost Island and see if our decoy is still at the bottom of the lake. If it's gone, maybe there'll be another clue, like more footprints in the mud or marks from the boat. That way when we go to the police, we'll have more info."

The bus rolled into Cabin Creek the next morning. While waiting for Uncle Wyatt in front of the Lodge, the cousins peeked in the chef's kitchen. The door was open and they could feel a rush of heat from the ovens.

"Hello, Mr. Henry," they called. The chef's face was flushed below his tall white hat. The sleeves of his white coat were rolled up. But when he saw the kids, he quickly pushed the sleeves down to his wrists. Then smiling, he wiped his hands on his apron.

"Come! See what I have on the cooling racks. A special treat for my friends." He gave them each a brownie on a paper doily.

"Thank you!"

He waved them off. "Nothing. It's nothing, I tell you. I loved making them at the café, remember? Now I always have to bake fancy desserts for the Lodge." The chef sighed. "You should run along. If Miss Allen sees me chatting and giving away food again, she'll never give me a raise. Oh, how I need some time away. With the air conditioner broken it seems I can't do anything right. I wish she would get it fixed — dear me, I shouldn't be telling you my troubles. I'm sorry, children. Now do run along."

An hour before sunset, the cousins paddled to Lost Island with their dogs. At the small cove, they looked into the rippling water. The sack lay bunched on the bottom.

"There it is!" they yelled. "Still here! Tied with our special triple knot."

Jeff picked up his oar and started sculling, turning for home. "*That* was lucky!" he said. "Now we can keep watch all summer."

The canoe glided across the lake. The cousins were glad they hadn't missed a chance to see the thief. And the dogs seemed glad to be with the kids again. Tessie, Rascal, and Yum-Yum sat quietly looking around.

David was in the bow. Finally, the moment had come.

"Guys?" he said. "I found an important clue. But it's . . . kinda . . ." He didn't finish his sentence. With a heavy heart he set his oar down, unzipped his pack, then opened the velvet case.

He turned around to look at Claire and Jeff. When they saw the handsome knife glinting in the sunlight, they both gasped with surprise.

"What? Where? Whose?" they both asked at once.

While David was telling his story, Rascal wiggled over to investigate. His little black nose started to sniff the blade.

"No, Rascal! It's sharp!" David jerked his hand away. The knife flipped up into the air. As if in slow motion, the treasure twisted and turned, falling, falling. With a heavy splash, it sank beyond his reach. Before he realized what had happened, the shining blade had disappeared in the dark deep.

The cousins stared after it, silent.

David could not believe what he had just done. *Why didn't I wait until we got home?* Even though he was ten years old, he wanted to cry. He felt ashamed.

"Was that the important clue, David?" Claire's voice was soft. "It was in the duffel with the other stuff?"

But his brother yelled. "David! How come you didn't —"

"Sorry . . . I'm sorry!" David cried. He put his hands over his ears and squeezed his eyes shut. After a moment he picked up his oar.

The cousins paddled home without speaking. David was miserable. But it wasn't just the lost knife that made him feel sick inside.

There was something else he needed to tell them.

12

The Mystery Deepens

The cousins tied up the canoe and went into the Bridger cabin. David retrieved his sketchbook from upstairs and took it into the sunroom. It was suppertime, so Jeff was making peanut butter sandwiches on the coffee table. Claire was peeling oranges and arranging them on a plate like a star. They looked up at David.

"What's wrong?" they asked.

David took a deep breath. Then he thumbed through his drawings. When he came to the knife, he showed them. It was the moment he'd been dreading.

"Wow," said Claire. "That's a chef's knife, like my dad's. Was all that stuff engraved on it?"

"Yes. On both sides of the handle. See?"

Jeff was confused. "So?"

"Well," said David, "remember when we got back from the ranch this morning?"

"Yeah."

"And we visited Chef Henry in the Lodge kitchen? It was hot, and his sleeves were rolled up."

Jeff's eyes widened as he slowly nodded his head. He looked at the drawings again.

"Mr. Henry's tattoos!" he exclaimed. "The bear and moose are on one arm, the buffalo's on the other. Just like your sketches of the knife."

"Oh, no," said Claire. Her face was solemn.

"At first, I couldn't remember where I'd seen them," David said. "But now I do. Once when Chef Henry was cooking at the café, he spilled a jug of mustard all down the front of his jacket. He took it off to get a clean one. That's when I saw his tattoos. Otherwise his sleeves always cover his arms."

The sun was setting behind the island. As the cousins ate their sandwiches, they gazed out the wide window. They were quiet. Three days at the ranch had tired them out. They were also worried about their friend.

Mom had come home and was paying bills at the kitchen table, so the kids went outside to talk. They lowered their voices. The *chirr-chirr-chirr* of crickets made it seem as if the night were whispering.

"Even if the knife *did* belong to Chef Henry," Jeff began, "what does it prove? Maybe someone stole it *and* the silver."

"Then why didn't he report it?" asked Claire. "I know for sure that if Daddy lost *his*, he'd freak out. He told me that a chef's knife is like a baseball catcher's mitt. Real personal. Not just any ol' mitt will do."

David had an explanation. "Maybe Mr. Henry knows who stole it but doesn't want to get the person in trouble."

"*Or*," said Jeff, "Mr. Henry took the silver because Miss Allen won't give him a raise. He didn't report his missing knife because he hid it with the loot, and —"

"— and then," Claire interrupted, "he

would have it with him when he escaped town with the silver. Daddy says a chef needs his special knife to get a new job. So if Miss Allen saw him carrying it out of the kitchen, she'd probably suspect he wasn't coming back."

David shook his head. "I can't believe this."

"Same here," said Jeff.

"Well, who else could it be?" Claire counted on her fingers. "It seems like Miss Allen, Rex, and Chef Henry all need money. They all work at the Lodge. They probably know about Theodore Roosevelt and his fancy gifts."

It was now dark out and getting cold on the porch. The cousins zipped up their sweatshirts. Through the window they could see the boys' mom in the kitchen making a cup of tea.

"I like Chef Henry," Claire said. "He's too nice to be a thief. I think Miss Allen and the McCoy boys are partners. They're the mean ones."

Suddenly, David started flipping through his sketchbook. "Guys, I just remembered something else." In the window light, he showed them his drawing of the day-camp picnic at the park.

It looked exactly as they had seen it, with balloons all over the playground and the clown with his hula hoop. Claire and Jeff studied the drawing.

"So?" they asked him.

David pointed to his sketch of Chef Henry in his tall white hat. He was standing at the barbecue. His feet and pant legs looked dirty.

"Mud." David was whispering. "It was all over his shoes. I didn't think anything of it till just this second. The park wasn't muddy."

"Wait!" Claire tried to keep her voice low. "The footprints! Out on the beach at Lost Island."

"*Yeah*," Jeff said slowly.

The cousins looked at the drawing again.

"Chef Henry's our friend," David said. "Do we have to go to the police right away?"

The cousins sat on the dark porch, looking at the stars. They were thinking.

Jeff broke the silence. "Well . . . maybe we can wait a bit. Keep an eye on the lake for that boat and see if anything else happens."

13

The Long Night

After dinner, Claire set up her telescope on the beach and pointed it at Lost Island. This was their third night of camping onshore near their cabins.

"Ready," she told her cousins, who were rolling out sleeping bags and a dog blanket. Though the air was brisk, it was more exciting to watch for the thief here than from indoors.

A window upstairs glowed with yellow light

where the boys' mom was reading. David clicked his walkie-talkie and turned a dial. "All's well, Mom," he said into the speaker. "Sweet dreams. Over."

"You, too. Stay safe, boys. Take care of Claire. Over."

Across the creek in the Posey cabin, Aunt Lilly and Uncle Wyatt were in their kitchen playing cards. Claire pushed a button on her walkie-talkie. "Night, Mom and Dad. See you at breakfast. Over."

A crackling voice answered. "We're here if you need us, honey. Be good to your cousins. Over."

As night fell, the lake sparkled with starlight. Waves washed in and out with a hush.

From the woods came the *whooo . . . whooo* of an owl, and a chorus of crickets. The forest was dark. There was no moon.

Binoculars ready, telescope aimed, the kids zipped themselves into their down sleeping bags. Warm against the cold breeze, they listened and waited. Tessie, Rascal, and Yum-Yum were curled up together, eyes closed.

Suddenly, Jeff noticed the Big Dipper had moved across the sky with all the other stars. It was the middle of the night! Hours had passed. When he heard the *putt . . . putt . . . putt* of an outboard motor far off on the lake, he shook his brother's arm.

"David," he whispered. "Claire. We fell asleep!"

*   *   *

A high-powered light was at the tip of the island. Someone was shining it into the water from a boat.

"Is it Rex McCoy?" they asked one another. Their hearts were beating fast.

Squinting through her telescope, Claire said, "Hold on a second. Rex doesn't have long hair. Look . . . is it Miss Allen?"

Jeff and David were focusing their binoculars. The boat was now beached. Someone was walking into the woods with a light, then disappeared in the shadows.

"Now she's heading to the fort!" Claire cried.

"Then we should get out there right now!" David began snapping on his life preserver, which he had been using for a pillow.

"Wait," said his older brother. "What would we do when we got there?"

"The dogs will protect us," David answered.

"No way," said Claire. "They're not budging. Look." In the starlight, they could see the blanket with three furry lumps. Not even Rascal had lifted a curious head.

Meanwhile, on Lost Island, the light swung high and low through the pine trees. Then, suddenly, it swung toward the cousins like a glowing eye.

"Duck!" Jeff cried.

They flattened themselves on the beach. For ten long seconds they hugged the cold sand. Finally, they peeked. The light had turned away from them and was bouncing through the woods again.

Claire jumped up to her telescope. "Now she's back in the boat! Look, there's a shiny blue stripe on its side."

The brothers followed the intruder with their binoculars.

"But why was she walking around? And why didn't she swim for the bag?" David asked.

"Probably just making sure it's still there," said Jeff. "As long as the thief thinks the loot is at the bottom of the lake, we have more time to find him. Or her."

Claire put the lens cap on her telescope. "What if it really is Miss Allen? If we go to the Lodge first thing tomorrow, maybe we can figure out who owns the boat with the blue stripe."

14

New Clues

The Blue Mountain Lodge resembled a huge log cabin. It had many wings, and porches that overlooked the lake. Window boxes were pretty with daisies, buttercups, and purple pansies. Every summer the shutters and doors were given a fresh coat of blue paint.

Next door to the Lodge was a cottage for the employees to use as a break room. It had a small kitchen, lockers, and cupboards for storage. In front of this cottage, the cousins noticed a teenager and a younger boy on step-ladders. They had cans and brushes and were wearing overalls with painters' caps. The boys looked familiar.

Riding closer, the kids realized it was the McCoy brothers.

Claire lifted Yum-Yum from her basket. She whispered, "Let's see if we can find out something from them."

"Good idea," said Jeff. "Hi there, Rex," he called. "Hi, Ronald. What's up?"

"What's it look like, shrimp? We're working! Some of us have responsibilities, you know."

"That's right!" said nine-year-old Ronald. "We have a summer job and you don't. *Na, na, na.*"

Holding Yum-Yum in her arms, Claire looked up the ladder at Rex. Her ponytail stuck out the back of her baseball cap. It bounced when she talked. She got right down to business.

"Are you guys partners with Miss Allen?" she asked. "We saw you shaking hands last week."

Rex gave her a dirty look. "What's it to you?"

"We have our reasons."

"Is that so!" cried Rex. "For your info, the manager pays us minimum wage. That's it. No pizza or sodas, and we have to wear these stupid uniforms. Plus there's the hot sun, mosquitoes, and nosy little pipsqueaks like you. We're not partners. It's slave labor."

The cousins looked at one another.

"So Miss Allen hired you?" Jeff asked.

"You got it. I'm broke. Need the money. My dad gave me a six o'clock curfew until I buy him a new engine for his fishing boat. Being a busboy pays squat, same with the army surplus store."

"So you weren't out on the lake last night?" Claire asked.

"Very funny," said Rex. "I'm grounded with no boat and no money to buy gas, and you think I'm out joyriding? Now beat it. Miss Allen will be coming back from her lunch any minute to check on us. And take that ugly little dog with you."

The cousins wandered around the Marina, looking at the small sailboats and dinghies. Canoes and kayaks were also tied up at the dock. The diesel engine of a cruiser churned the water as it left for a sightseeing tour.

"Hey!" David pointed to an aluminum boat with a shiny blue stripe on its side. "Is that the one from last night?"

"Sure looks like it!" cried Jeff.

But just then, an identical boat motored from the lake into the small harbor. It, too, had a blue stripe. A woman was steering, laughing as if she were having fun. Her hair blew off her shoulders from the breeze. A man next to her was smiling.

Jeff said, "Isn't that Miss Allen?"

"Yep," Claire replied. "And who's that with her? He looks familiar."

"And which boat was at the island last night?" David began sketching the two craft in his notebook, hoping to notice a detail that would be a clue. He was glad he always carried the pad in his pack.

They watched Miss Allen and her companion tie up at the dock, then get out with a picnic basket. As they walked toward the employee cottage, they held hands and gazed into each other's eyes. The cousins had never seen her look so happy and carefree. But there was something else unusual about Miss Allen.

"She's wearing hiking boots," Claire remarked. "Big clunkers. Those are big enough to have left the prints on the beach."

Jeff crossed his arms, thinking. "Okay. Here's another theory. Since Rex is grounded, the only suspects who could've been out there last night are Chef Henry and Miss Allen."

"But there was only one person in the boat," said David. "And that person had long hair."

"Wait!" said Claire. "What if Miss Allen and Chef are really friends and they just *pretend* to fight? They could've been planning this robbery for a long time so they can run away together and open their own restaurant. That's what Mom and Dad did. Well, they didn't rob a bank or anything, but when they got married they moved to Cabin Creek and started the Western Café."

Jeff nodded toward the path. "But that guy with the picnic basket seems like a boyfriend. Are *they* pretending, too?"

"Well," Claire answered slowly, as she thought of possibilities, "*maybe* the boyfriend is a decoy. Like our sack of rocks. I wish I could remember where I've seen him. Anyway, if he and Miss Allen are acting romantic, no one will suspect that she and Chef are the real partners."

David tapped his pencil on his drawing.

"Guys, the only difference between these boats is the numbers on the side. See? Below the stripes? *Blue Mountain Lodge 3* and *Blue Mountain Lodge 4*. There're probably two others just like these."

"Good eye, buddy!" Jeff said. "Now all we have to do is find out who else is allowed to use these boats."

Waiting Out the Storm

As the cousins walked along the wharf, the sky suddenly went dark. Black thunderheads swept over the mountains and hid the sun. The air felt wet.

"Storm!" David cried. "And it's coming fast."

When lightning flickered through the clouds, Jeff yelled, "Let's get away from the water!" Their parents often warned them about how water could attract lightning.

A few seconds later, there was a loud crack of thunder. At the same moment, wind rushed over the lake. Boats tied up at the docks bounced in the choppy water.

"Hurry!" cried Claire, picking up Yum-Yum and holding her tight.

Just as rain began pelting them, they reached the Lodge's protected entrance. Tourists were running up the steps, holding newspapers or shopping bags over their heads against the sudden downpour.

Inside was the great room. Tall ceilings made from huge logs crisscrossed overhead with iron chandeliers. The stone fireplace was large enough to fit a small car and was blazing with a cozy fire. Mounted over the mantel was the buffalo head Mr. Wellback had told them about. It was enormous. Horns curled above its ears. They wondered if Theodore Roosevelt had hunted it.

Yum-Yum growled at the dark fur and glass eyes. "Shh," said Claire. "It won't hurt you."

The cousins liked it here and came often to read magazines while waiting for Claire's parents. They gazed around at the reading chairs, at the long leather couches and love seats where people were sitting with books or talking. There was a pleasant hubbub of voices. Many were watching the storm from a wall of windows that reached from the floor to the ceiling. The lake was bumpy with whitecaps.

"Hey, guys, look." Claire pointed to an empty display case that stood in a corner of the room. There was a large WET PAINT sign taped to the glass. "They must've moved this from another room. We've never seen it before." Inside the case was an announcement. David read it aloud.

To our visitors.

Please excuse our missing treasures. Due to our summer painting project, all historical artifacts are temporarily in storage. Thank you for your patience.

The Management, Blue Mountain Lodge

"Well, that explains a lot," said Jeff. "I wonder where the treasures are supposed to be stored."

Claire leaned close to the boys. "Let's ask Miss Allen. Maybe she'll seem guilty and give away another clue."

Gift shops lined one side of the great room. There were a lunch counter and bookstore. The opposite side opened up to the elegant dining room, where the cousins now headed. Miss Allen was at the cash register, answering the phone. She had changed into her work clothes and was wearing her dainty black shoes. This time her long hair was brushed back and held by a pretty clip, and her cheeks were rosy from being outside.

"Chef," she called into the kitchen. Her

voice was kind and she looked worried. "Long distance. I hope everything's all right. It's your sister again."

The children ducked into a seating area nearby, where Mr. Henry couldn't see them.

"Yes, I will come as soon as I can," he said into the telephone. "But, Sis, I made a terrible mistake" — his voice was drowned out by a baby shrieking in a passing stroller. The cousins strained to listen — "tried to fix it . . . but . . . am in trouble . . ."

At this, the cousins exchanged glances and slipped away. They went to the lunch counter and ordered orangeade and grilled hot dogs. They whispered.

"Chef Henry sounded really upset!"

"What did he mean by a terrible mistake? And what kind of trouble is he in?"

"And what did he try to fix? Sounds to me like he's the thief."

When a teenage waitress brought their food, Claire asked if it was fun working at the Lodge.

"It's totally cool," the girl answered. She was about sixteen and had several tiny hoops in each ear. Her eyelashes were dark with mascara. "I only work three days a week, but they let us use the paddleboats and they take us out wakeboarding, stuff like that."

"What about those motorboats?" David asked. "The ones with the Lodge's name?"

The girl rolled her eyes. "I *wish*. But only full-time employees are allowed to. Hey, I gotta get another order. Holler if you need anything else."

Jeff spooned pickle relish onto his plate,

then onto Claire's. He said, "Miss Allen and Chef Henry work full-time, right?"

"Right." Claire gave Jeff some of her fries and took his lettuce leaf. "But not Rex."

David's brow was furrowed in thought. He didn't notice his brother piling chopped onion on his hot dog. "Since Chef Henry is our friend," David said, "shouldn't we ask him about all this? If he's innocent, then we can go to the police."

"But if he's not?" Claire asked.

Neither boy answered.

16

Another Puzzle

Finally, the storm passed. The cousins paid the cashier for their lunch, then went outside. The grass and flowers sparkled from the rain, and once again the sun was hot. They noticed Chef Henry at the kitchen door, taking a break.

"You'll be sorry!" he yelled to someone inside. He began pacing back and forth along the dirt path.

"He seems nervous," Jeff said. "Still think we should talk to him?"

Claire and David hesitated. "Well —"

"How could you be so careless?" came a woman's voice from the kitchen. It was Miss Allen's.

"*Me?*" the chef yelled. "That's a laugh. Maybe if *you* weren't so . . ." The chef's words were lost as he turned away. That's when the cousins noticed something had slipped from underneath the edge of his hat and down his neck. It was a ponytail, about six inches long.

Without saying a word, they ran to their bikes and rode home through the woods.

"He has long hair!" they kept saying to one another in disbelief.

"Maybe *he* was on the lake the other night, looking in the water!"

"So what're we supposed to do now?" they asked one another.

"First, let's go to Lost Island," said Jeff, "and check our decoy. Then we'll haul everything to the police. They'll know what to do."

The canoe drifted near the tip of the island. David looked down over the bow to the sandy bottom. Jeff looked over the stern. Claire looked from both sides. Their oars rippled the clear water.

"It's gone."

"But when? It was here yesterday."

"Probably last night. We must've slept through the whole thing!"

The cousins looked at their dogs for someone to blame. "They didn't wake us up," David said. "They've been sleeping on the job!"

Back home, they tied their canoe to the dock. They were still shocked about Mr. Henry's long hair and wondered what kind of trouble he was in. As they walked up to the Bridger cabin they heard a ringing telephone. Jeff ran into the kitchen to answer, then a moment later returned outside.

"That was Mom," he said. "Uncle Wyatt'll be here in ten minutes to pick us up. There's a bluegrass band in the park so we're supposed to meet her there. Aunt Lilly's packing a picnic supper for all of us." Jeff sighed. "Guess we can't go to the police until tomorrow."

While waiting on the porch for Uncle Wyatt, they discussed the clues.

"Okay," Jeff began. "So Chef Henry and Miss Allen both have long hair. And they both could have made those footprints. "

"They work at the Lodge full-time," added Claire, "so either one of them could have taken out one of those boats we saw."

"So it could be Chef Henry *or* Ms. Allen," David said. "Or it could be Chef Henry *and* Ms. Allen. They both need money, and they argue a lot."

Jeff nodded.

"They might only be pretending to fight and they're actually friends —"

"*Special* friends," Claire said, "who want to sell the loot so they can run away together and open up a restaurant. That's why they put Chef Henry's knife in with the silver."

David said, "Well, someone is probably furious after finding a duffel bag of rocks. I hope they don't come looking here."

Jeff bit his lip. He glanced at the upstairs window, shiny in the late afternoon sun. "All that silver is in our closet. We should've taken it to the cops a long time ago."

17

A Terrible Shock

The park was busy with children on the swings and jungle gym and with parents spreading blankets on the lawn for their picnic dinners. The musicians on stage were tapping their feet in time to banjos and fiddles. It was a festive summer evening.

Aunt Lilly waved when she saw the cousins looking for her. "Over here, kids!" she called.

Uncle Wyatt brought a card table from his jeep. He had sawed off the legs so it stood five inches from the ground. Soon their supper of pastrami sandwiches, pickles, and coleslaw was arranged on paper plates. Mom opened a bag of tortilla chips and a jar of salsa. The two families sat together on the grass.

"Any new adventures today?" asked Mom.

Claire sat up straight and smiled. "We love summer!" she exclaimed with all her heart. It was her way of avoiding the real story.

"How 'bout that terrific thundershower this afternoon?" Uncle Wyatt said. "Boys, your dad always loved a good rainstorm. Said it stirs the soul."

Jeff and David liked hearing stories about their father. The families talked on. For dessert, Aunt Lilly removed some tinfoil from a plate and passed around fresh oatmeal cookies.

Then she waved to someone over at the picnic pavilion.

"There's our Henry," she said. "Looks like he's cooking for those Swedish visitors. They're staying at the Lodge and came to the café for breakfast —"

"Chef Henry's *here*?" the cousins said in unison. They turned to see him standing at the barbecue pit. "May we please be excused?"

"Of course. Take your time. The band's playing until sunset."

As the kids walked across the grassy field, they whispered among themselves.

"Should we ask him any questions?"

"What should we say?"

Mr. Henry saw them and smiled. "Hello," he called. "Are you hungry? There's plenty here."

"Thank you. We've already eaten."

Claire's eyes fell to the chef's feet. She caught her breath. His shoes were once again covered in globs of mud. Jeff and David nudged each other.

"Your poor shoes," said Claire. She wasn't sure how to start this conversation.

"Oh," the chef replied. "It's that sprinkler again. It goes off right where I park the van to unload groceries at the Lodge. It's been leaking for weeks, but I always forget and walk right into that gooey puddle."

The cousins gave one another a knowing look. So, it *was* possible that Chef Henry hadn't been on the island the previous night. David took his sketchbook from his pack. He found the drawing of day camp and showed him.

"My, you're a good artist, young man. I remember that morning well — all those kids,

and that obnoxious clown. He kept squirting my shoes with a water pistol. I was
upset because it splashed mud onto my white
pants."

"So you stepped in the puddle that day,
too?" Claire asked.

"I'm afraid so," the chef answered. "That's
one reason Miss Allen is so mad at me. She
says I'm careless and sloppy and ruining the
Lodge's lawn." He turned to the grill and, with
his spatula, flipped sixteen hamburger patties,
two at a time. "What else do you have in your
book there?"

David hesitated. When his brother and
Claire gave him a nod, he thumbed through
the pages to the knife.

The man gasped. "Where'd you see this?"

"We found it."

"Oh, that's good news!" the chef cried. "Where —"

"— but we lost it. Actually, *I* lost it." David started to explain what had happened, but a worried look from his brother silenced him. They still didn't know if the chef was involved in the robbery.

Mr. Henry seemed to understand there was more to David's story. He took a deep breath. "You probably want to know how I lost this beautiful knife. Dear me, this is difficult. I'm ashamed to say I'm in a bit of trouble. This is no excuse, but my sister in New York is sick. I've been trying to save money to go back and take care of her, but Miss Allen has never given me a raise and she won't give me time off. It seems we get into more arguments with every passing week. We used to be good friends."

"But, Chef Henry, what does that have to do with your knife?"

"Well, I've been working overtime. Lots. I'm so tired that I keep making mistakes. First, I broke a crystal punch bowl — it just slipped out of my hands. Then it was some wineglasses. It's not like me to be so clumsy, but Miss Allen said I had to pay for everything, and that if I broke or lost one more item, she'd tell the owners to fire me. Then on top of all this, I messed up the Lodge's lasagna recipe. Somehow my tomato sauce was full of tiny cinnamon candies. Was I so tired that I mixed up the ingredients? I don't know, but *that's* why I didn't report my knife missing. She would accuse me again of being careless. I need my job. It's a lot more stressful than when I worked with your folks at the café. Now, those were the days. They treated me like family. Still do."

Mr. Henry took a handkerchief from his pocket and wiped his brow. "I shouldn't have burdened you children with all this. Once again, please forgive me."

Jeff had one more question for their friend. "Chef Henry, do you ever have any free time to do fun stuff, like take a boat out on the lake?"

"Time!" He laughed. "Even if I did, I wouldn't dare. I never learned to swim, and I'm scared to death of deep water. Well, I need to serve up these burgers. Good night, you three."

"Good night, Chef."

❊ ❊ ❊

The backseat windows were rolled down to the cool night air as Uncle Wyatt drove them home. He was singing to the radio, so the children were able to whisper without his hearing them.

"I can't wait for tomorrow."

"Me, neither. We'll turn in the stuff to the cops and tell them about Miss Allen."

"And we won't have to worry about it anymore!"

Uncle Wyatt pulled up to the Bridger cabin. He went in to make sure everything was all right and to let the dogs out for a few minutes. He put Claire's sleeping bag and pillow in the sunroom, where the kids were going to camp. This was a summer tradition, having a sleepover when both sets of parents worked late.

"Well, sweetheart, back to the café." Uncle Wyatt hugged her. "Tonight we're open till midnight, so see you all tomorrow." As usual, he waved his cowboy hat to his nephews before driving away.

"Let's watch a movie! I'll get the popcorn started," Claire volunteered.

"Good idea," said Jeff. "David, let's get everything together for tomorrow." The boys raced each other upstairs, followed by the three dogs.

But soon Claire heard them yelling.

"Claire, hurry!"

"Get up here!"

She ran up two steps at a time, arriving in their room out of breath. The brothers and dogs were staring into the closet.

It was empty.

18

A Frantic Search

The cousins were too shocked to speak. The only sound was the *poppity-pop-pop* from the microwave downstairs. The dogs had stopped wagging their tails. Their ears were perked up as if waiting for an explanation.

Finally, Claire said, "What happened?"

The brothers shook their heads. "No idea."

Claire studied the scene. As usual, David's bed was messy and his shoes were scattered around the floor with wadded-up socks. Jeff's quilt, however, was neatly tucked in, his flip-flops and shoes organized in a row beneath his bed.

"Your room looks the same," she said, "except someone scooped everything out of your closet. Even the clothes are gone."

Jeff held out his palms, a bewildered look on his face. "I don't get it. If Mom was up here cleaning, why didn't she say something to us at dinner?"

"I'll call the animal hospital and ask her," said David. He ran into her room to use the phone. "Hello? May I speak to Dr. Bridger,

please? Oh . . . in surgery? Just a moment."
He looked across the hallway to Jeff and Claire.
Is this an emergency? he mouthed.

"No!" they said, waving their hands.

"No, it's not an emergency. Thank you, anyway." David hung up.

"Is anything else in the house missing?"
Claire asked.

"Our binoculars are still here," said Jeff.
"Plus my bug collection and fossils. Weird. I
wonder who else knew what was hidden in our
closet."

"Mr. Wellback."

"But he's our friend. He wouldn't break
in here."

"Right."

"Maybe the thief was sloppy and left a clue,"
Jeff offered. "I'll start looking up here."

Claire and David hurried downstairs to search. The dogs followed them from room to room. When a cupboard was opened they poked their whiskered noses inside, sniffing. Nothing seemed out of place.

After twenty minutes, the brothers plopped down in the sunroom. Jeff said, "I can't believe we went to all that trouble getting those things out of the lake, and now someone's swiped them."

Just then, Claire scrambled out of the kitchen. She had found something under the breakfast nook. "Look at this, guys. A clue!" she said, holding up a piece of paper. "Some kind of note." She read it aloud.

Hey, Dr. Bridger. Alls I had time for today was one upstairs closet. Boy, did it stink.

Don't worry, everything's washed and in the laundry area with all the puzzles and games, etc. You said to donate any junk, so am dropping some stuff off. Thanks for the job. Be back next week. See ya, Tiffany

"Who's Tiffany?" David asked.

"Who cares!" said his brother. "Let's look in the garage."

They flicked on the light.

The Volkswagen Bug that had belonged to their father was parked on one side. Cluttered around it were bikes and ski equipment, camping gear and soccer balls. A lawn mower was pushed up against a fifty-pound bag of dog food. The cousins searched the many shelves stocked with canned goods and picnic supplies. They found some puzzles and games from their closet. Against one wall were the washer and dryer, where the boys' clothes were now folded.

There was no sign of the silver bowls or platters.

"We're gonna be thrown in the slammer for this," David moaned.

Jeff sat down on an ice chest, his chin in his hand. "The next time we find something that's not ours, we're turning it in *right away*. Okay, guys?"

"Definitely!"

Sitting at the kitchen nook, Claire searched through the yellow pages of a telephone book.

David's pencil was ready to write down an address. Jeff hunted through their recycle bin for clues to any donation centers. He also tried to find a number for Tiffany.

"Salvation Army," Claire read from the Thrift Shop section. *"Double Duty Duds . . . Second Time Around . . .* There're eight stores here! How do we know where Tiffany went?"

David had an idea. "Even though it's late, let's call all these places. Maybe a recording will say when they open. Then tomorrow we'll just go to each one."

The cousins took turns. Three stores had a recorded message saying they were no longer in business. David crossed them off his list.

"Five more to go," said Claire.

"Thrifty Threads is remodeling," said a cheerful voice, *"so we'll be closed until —"*

Jeff hung up the phone. "Four more."

Claire dialed another number. *"We're sorry, but New to You is no longer accepting donations, so please —"*

David crossed that one off. "Three left," he said.

Finally, they had their list. David drew a quick map showing the locations with their hours: 9:30 A.M. until 4:30 P.M.

"Good thinking, buddy," said Jeff. He gave his brother and Claire a high five. "Okay, there's still time for a movie, but tomorrow we better get an early start."

"Eight o'clock sharp," said David.

Claire took their bag of popcorn from the microwave. "Mission Recovery, part two," she said.

19

The Locker

All night, the cousins were too restless to sleep.

When they finally heard a robin singing through the open window, they crawled out of their sleeping bags. It was five o'clock in the morning.

They would tell Mom about everything later. But for now they wrote her a note and crept out to the porch for their bikes. As they took the shortcut to town, the forest came alive with chittering birds and squirrels. The rising sun spread fingers of light through the trees and across their path.

They arrived at Tammy's Treasures at ten minutes after six, more than three hours before it would open.

"Boy, are we early!" said Jeff. He leaned over the handlebars of his bike to read David's map. "Let's ride by the other places for a look."

Claire led the way, down Second Street to Oak. At Benny & June's they peeked in the windows, but it was too dark to see anything. They rode on to Third Street, stopping at the corner shop on Maple. There on the side-walk was a large wooden box with a sign: DONATIONS.

Jeff and David lifted its heavy lid. Inside was a large trash bag. The brothers first poked it. Then, when they heard a familiar rattle, they tore it open.

"Awesome!" David yelled. "We're not going to the slammer after all."

"It's all here!" cried Jeff.

Claire had planned ahead and brought three laundry bags with drawstrings at the top. Into these, the cousins carefully put every bowl and platter, then balanced them on their bikes for the ride to the police station.

The captain was drinking his first cup of coffee as he listened to the cousins.

"This is some story," he said, after thanking them for turning everything in. "There's no proof Miss Allen is guilty, but we can certainly ask her a few questions. Problem is, today I'm shorthanded, so I won't make it to the Lodge until later this morning."

Chef Henry was busy baking two hundred cupcakes for a child's birthday party that day. There would be pony rides at the Lodge corral, a clown, and barbecued hot dogs.

"Morning, Chef," the cousins said at the kitchen door. Now that they knew he wasn't the thief, they were eager to give him a friendly hello.

"Glad to see you!" he called to them.

The cousins locked their bikes at the Marina, where there was a little grocery store. They bought orange juice and donuts, then sat under a pine tree. It was near the cottage that the Lodge employees used for their breaks.

As the kids were eating their breakfast, they

heard loud voices from inside. They listened and were surprised to hear Miss Allen arguing with a man. This time, it wasn't Chef Henry.

"Did you take my keys again?" she asked.

"There you go, always accusing me," said the man.

"Come on, Bob, I'm going to be late. Where are they?"

"Right there on the counter, are you blind? I've gotta work, too, you know. Another stupid birthday party full of spoiled rich kids. I don't know how much longer I can take being around all these brats."

The cottage door opened and a man stormed past the cousins and down the woodsy path. When he turned around to glare at Miss Allen, they recognized him.

"The boyfriend," Jeff whispered.

"*Bob* the boyfriend," said David.

"Bob the *clown*," Claire said, also whispering. "Now I remember where I've seen him. At day camp. He didn't wear face paint or anything, just a funny orange wig and a red nose."

A few minutes later, Miss Allen left, wearing her nice black shoes. She was carrying a soggy tissue and her eyes were red. She left the door wide open.

As soon as the kids finished their juice, they crept to the doorway. They noticed that one of the tall lockers was slightly open. A piece of canvas hung out the bottom.

David said, "Guys, think it's okay if we go in?"

Claire answered by marching inside. When she brushed past the canvas, dirt and pebbles sprinkled to the floor. It was the duffel bag sliced open in the middle, with the boys' famous triple knot still holding the top closed.

"Uh-oh," she said, now pointing to a pair of hiking boots, "is this Miss Allen's locker?"

Now all three cousins were in the cottage. They could see a small shelf in the locker, where there was a box of cinnamon candies and a bottle of olive oil.

David leaned in to smell the candy. "Red Hots! I bet someone sneaked these in the tomato sauce so it would ruin Chef's lasagna."

Jeff knew this was someone's personal locker, but he couldn't help himself. He touched the bottle, which was oily from a spill. He said, "Hey, what if Miss Allen smeared some of this on the punch bowl? It would be hard to hold, so maybe that's why Chef Henry dropped it."

The cousins stared at the duffel bag and hiking boots, trying to figure out why Miss Allen would want to cause trouble for the chef. That's when they noticed a plastic water pistol. When Jeff knelt down for a closer look, he saw something else.

A wig with long orange hair.

"Whoa," said Jeff, "I think this is the clown's locker."

"*Bob* the Clown," said David.

"Bob the *Thief*," Claire corrected.

20

One Last Question

In front of the Lodge, a crowd of tourists gathered near the police car. They craned their necks to see who was being arrested, but eventually, one by one, they wandered away.

Miss Allen stood with the cousins, watching. Her eyes were red from crying, but her face was brave.

Bob was in handcuffs, in the back of the squad car. The captain was still interviewing him.

"So why did you try to set up the chef?" he asked.

"The guy's a beginner," Bob said, angry. He was glad someone was listening to his complaints. "We both applied for the job here, but the owners hired him instead of me. *I'm* the one who went to culinary arts school in Paris. Henry's just a cook from the Western Café. A burger flipper. Tattoo man. A nobody. He can't even make a decent flambé. And I've been stuck clowning around for two years."

The captain was writing on a clipboard. "Let's go over this again. You took Miss Allen's keys to the storage cupboard. Then you stole the treasures that had been given to our town by President Theodore Roosevelt —"

"Lousy politician," Bob interrupted.

"— then you stole the chef's knife," the captain continued, "so that it would keep him from doing a good job, thus ruining his career. Then you planned to sell everything — for what purpose?"

"To get out of town!" Bob cried from the backseat. "What d'you think?"

"And take Miss Allen with you?"

"That was my first plan — to hawk all the silver and go to Italy together — but then she started to get on my nerves. She and that cook were getting way too chummy."

"So you were jealous. You wanted the chef out of the picture. You knew he has long hair, and that he wears it down when he's not at work, so you figured your clown wig would fool people. You assumed that if anyone saw you in the boat, they would see the hair and blame the chef. But then you changed your mind about running away with Miss Allen, didn't you? You decided to keep the loot for yourself. Do I have this right?"

"Oh, you're so smart, Captain."

The cousins heard Miss Allen whisper. "You *rat.*" Then she said, "You're not my boyfriend anymore! I'm glad the owners didn't hire you as head chef. And now that you won't be around to cause trouble, Henry can take the vacation he deserves."

"I'm too good for this place," Bob insisted.

The captain was almost finished. "Oh, yeah? Well, you must have been a sorry thief when you realized your treasure was nothing more than a pile of rocks."

"Oh, shut up."

"One last question. Why would a thief such as yourself get out of his boat to walk around an island in the middle of the night?"

Bob rolled his eyes. "*Hello?* To make sure no one was camping there. Didn't want any witnesses."

"Well, that about wraps it up." The captain clicked his pen and put it in his shirt pocket. To an officer standing guard he said, "Let's show this bum the inside of a jail cell."

At that, Claire picked up her backpack and turned to her cousins. "I've heard enough."

"Me, too," said David.

"Hey, guys," said Jeff, looking at the lake. "What d'you say we pack a lunch and head out to Fort Grizzly Paw? Who knows what we'll see from the lookout tower this time?"

GET A SNEAK PEEK AT
JEFF, DAVID, AND CLAIRE'S
NEXT EXCITING ADVENTURE:

THE LEGEND
OF SKULL CLIFF

1

The Cliff

Ten-year-old David Bridger stood near the edge of Skull Cliff, looking out at the vast lake and the distant range of mountains. It was windy this high up. He brushed his blond hair from his eyes. Then he kicked some gravel to see how far it would fly before dropping from sight. As usual, his socks were mismatched: one striped, one plain.

"Hey, Jeff," he said to his older brother. "What'd you think would happen if we slipped?"

"The cold water would knock us out," Jeff answered, pulling David away from the railing. He was twelve and cautious about such things. He and his brother wore T-shirts. Jeff's still had a crease from where it had been neatly folded in his drawer, but David's was inside out because he often dressed in a hurry.

"Remember those boys Dad told us about?" asked Jeff. "From when he was a kid?"

"Sorta."

"Well, they were goofing around up here and fell." Jeff reminded him. "Even though they knew how to swim, they sank and never came up."

David shivered. It was just one more spooky story about Skull Cliff. "Oh . . . yeah . . . I remember now. Then it's a good thing the dogs are safe at home. Except for *you-know-who*." He glanced at their cousin, Claire, who was holding a white poodle in her arms.

"Yum-Yum is perfectly safe. Don't worry," she replied, showing the sparkly pink leash wrapped around her hand. Claire Posey was nine. Her curly red hair was held back with a barrette that matched Yum-Yum's yellow collar. A pair of binoculars hung around Claire's neck. With her free hand she looked through them, adjusting the focus with a practiced thumb.

"I hope no one can see our fort from here," she said.

The brothers took their binoculars out of their backpacks. They scanned the lake with its many small islands, and also Grizzly Paw Wilderness — a remote stretch of land that surrounded the shoreline. On the far southern shore, the cousins saw their log homes and the beach where their families' boats were docked.

Lost Island was hidden in the farthest inlet. Just this summer, their parents had allowed them to explore it for the first time. Their secret clubhouse was on this forested isle. They had made the trip that morning to make sure no one could see their fort from the top of Skull Cliff.

"We're in luck," Jeff said. "No one will ever guess that tall tree is our lookout tower. You can't even see the platform."

A shout drew their attention to the dirt road leading up to the cliff.

"Uh-oh," said Claire. "Here they come. No more peace and quiet."

An old blue bus was unloading by the picnic

area. Painted on its side was the CAMP WHIS-PERING PINES logo that pictured a log cabin with pine trees. Already, kids were chasing one another around clumps of sagebrush and yelling at the top of their lungs. Two boys began sword fighting with twigs.

One of the counselors blew his whistle. He was holding a clipboard and wore a T-shirt with a logo that matched the bus. "People!" he called. "It's ten o'clock so we'll start the hike in fifteen minutes. Since this is our third hike this week, you should remember the rules." He was now shouting to be heard.

"Stay on the trail, people! Don't pick any wildflowers! Do not tease the chipmunks! And no throwing pinecones like last time! You could poke someone's eye out!"

Jeff and David gave each other satisfied

looks. They knew all this. Their father had been a forest ranger before he died last winter, and had taught them well. He had loved showing city kids the mountains and how to respect nature. In fact, his love for the wilderness had begun when he himself was a child at Camp Whispering Pines. Jeff had his dad's brown hair and deep brown eyes.

After some moments of watching the campers, Jeff suddenly craned his neck, looking behind and around him. "Where's Claire?" His voice was urgent. "She never goes anywhere without telling us."

"Uh . . . don't know. She was right here."

"Claire!" they called, trying to spot their cousin among the crowd.

Knowing the history of the cliff, the boys grew nervous when they didn't see her. They turned toward the overhang. Without saying anything, they crept forward. Once at the railing, they peered over the rim, down to the ice-blue lake. David's stomach twirled from the dizzying height. Jeff no longer felt brave. With their binoculars, they began searching the water, hoping Claire and her little white poodle had not slipped from the edge.

"She's always so careful," Jeff said. "But what if she fell?"

"We better call for help!" David unhooked his walkie-talkie from his belt.

"What are you guys doing?" came a voice behind them.

The brothers whipped around. "Claire!" they cried.

"Hey," she said, uncertain why they were so excited to see her. "You won't believe this kid from Whispering Pines," she said. "He wants to buy Yum-Yum because he's lonesome for his dog at home. He tried to give me a fifty-dollar bill."

"That's crazy!" David exclaimed, still relieved to see that Claire was safe.

Claire shrugged her shoulders. "I know. The kid claims camp is boring so he's going to make some fun of his own."

"That doesn't sound good," Jeff said. As the oldest, most responsible cousin, he was now worried. Jeff returned his gaze to the icy water beneath Skull Cliff, then to the expanse of wilderness beyond the lake. His dad had taught him that nature provided all the excitement a kid could need — and sometimes more.